Title

AF113457

Themes

Prompt

Setting

Message

Protagonist

Name

Driving Goal

Obstacle or Conflict

Get writing!

Word Count _____

Title

Themes

Prompt

Setting

Message

Protagonist

Name

Driving Goal

Obstacle or Conflict

Get writing!

Word Count _____

Title

Themes

Prompt

Setting

Message

Protagonist

Name

Driving Goal

Obstacle or Conflict

Get writing!

Word Count _____

Title

Themes

Prompt

Setting

Message

Protagonist

Name

Driving Goal

Obstacle or Conflict

Get writing!

Word Count _____

Title

Themes

Prompt

Setting

Message

Protagonist

Name

Driving Goal

Obstacle or Conflict

Get writing!

Word Count

Title

Themes

Prompt

Setting

Message

Protagonist

Name

Driving Goal

Obstacle or Conflict

Get writing!

Word Count _____

Title

Themes

Prompt

Setting

Message

Protagonist

Name

Driving Goal

Obstacle or Conflict

Get writing!

Word Count

Title

Themes

Prompt

Setting

Message

Protagonist

Name

Driving Goal

Obstacle or Conflict

Get writing!

Word Count _____

Title

Themes

Prompt

Setting

Message

Protagonist

Name

Driving Goal

Obstacle or Conflict

Get writing!

Word Count _____

Title

Themes

Prompt

Setting

Message

Protagonist

Name

Driving Goal

Obstacle or Conflict

Get writing!

Word Count _____

Title

Themes

Prompt

Setting

Message

Protagonist

Name

Driving Goal

Obstacle or Conflict

Get writing!

Word Count

Title

Themes

Prompt

Setting

Message

Protagonist

Name

Driving Goal

Obstacle or Conflict

Get writing!

_____
_____
_____
_____
_____
_____
_____
_____
_____
_____
_____
_____
_____

Word Count _____

Title

Themes

Prompt

Setting

Message

Protagonist

Name

Driving Goal

Obstacle or Conflict

Get writing!

Word Count _____

Title

Themes

Prompt

Setting

Message

Protagonist

Name

Driving Goal

Obstacle or Conflict

Get writing!

Word Count _____

Title

Themes

Prompt

Setting

Message

Protagonist

Name

Driving Goal

Obstacle or Conflict

Get writing!

Word Count _____

Title

Themes

Prompt

Setting

Message

Protagonist

Name

Driving Goal

Obstacle or Conflict

Get writing!

_____
_____
_____
_____
_____
_____
_____
_____
_____
_____
_____
_____

Word Count _____

Title

Themes

Prompt

Setting

Message

Protagonist

Name

Driving Goal

Obstacle or Conflict

Get writing!

Word Count _____

Title

Themes

Prompt

Setting

Message

Protagonist

Name

Driving Goal

Obstacle or Conflict

Get writing!

Word Count _____

Title

Themes

Prompt

Setting

Message

Protagonist

Name

Driving Goal

Obstacle or Conflict

Get writing!

Word Count _____

Title

Themes

Prompt

Setting

Message

Protagonist

Name

Driving Goal

Obstacle or Conflict

Get writing!

Word Count _____

Title

Themes

Prompt

Setting

Message

Protagonist

Name

Driving Goal

Obstacle or Conflict

Get writing!

Word Count

Title

Themes

Prompt

Setting

Message

Protagonist

Name

Driving Goal

Obstacle or Conflict

Get writing!

Word Count _____

Title

Themes

Prompt

Setting

Message

Protagonist

Name

Driving Goal

Obstacle or Conflict

Get writing!

Word Count _____

Title

Themes

Prompt

Setting

Message

Protagonist

Name

Driving Goal

Obstacle or Conflict

Get writing!

_____
_____
_____
_____
_____
_____
_____
_____
_____
_____
_____
_____
_____
_____

Word Count _____

Title

Themes

Prompt

Setting

Message

Protagonist

Name

Driving Goal

Obstacle or Conflict

Get writing!

Word Count _____

Title

Themes

Prompt

Setting

Message

Protagonist

Name

Driving Goal

Obstacle or Conflict

Get writing!

Word Count _____

Title

Themes

Prompt

Setting

Message

Protagonist

Name

Driving Goal

Obstacle or Conflict

Get writing!

Word Count

Title

Themes

Prompt

Setting

Message

Protagonist

Name

Driving Goal

Obstacle or Conflict

Get writing!

Word Count _____

Title

Themes

Prompt

Setting

Message

Protagonist

Name

Driving Goal

Obstacle or Conflict

Get writing!

Word Count _____

Title

Themes

Prompt

Setting

Message

Protagonist

Name

Driving Goal

Obstacle or Conflict

Get writing!

Word Count _____

Title

Themes

Prompt

Setting

Message

Protagonist

Name

Driving Goal

Obstacle or Conflict

Get writing!

Word Count

Title

Themes

Prompt

Setting

Message

Protagonist

Name

Driving Goal

Obstacle or Conflict

Get writing!

Word Count _____

Title

Themes

Prompt

Setting

Message

Protagonist

Name

Driving Goal

Obstacle or Conflict

Get writing!

Word Count _____

Title

Themes

Prompt

Setting

Message

Protagonist

Name

Driving Goal

Obstacle or Conflict

Get writing!

Word Count _____

Title

Themes

Prompt

Setting

Message

Protagonist

Name

Driving Goal

Obstacle or Conflict

Get writing!

Word Count

Title

Themes

Prompt

Setting

Message

Protagonist

Name

Driving Goal

Obstacle or Conflict

Get writing!

Word Count _____

Title

Themes
Prompt

Setting

Message

Protagonist
Name

Driving Goal

Obstacle or Conflict

Get writing!

Word Count

Title

Themes

Prompt

Setting

Message

Protagonist

Name

Driving Goal

Obstacle or Conflict

Get writing!

Word Count _____

Title

Themes

Prompt

Setting

Message

Protagonist

Name

Driving Goal

Obstacle or Conflict

Get writing!

Word Count _____

Title

Themes

Prompt

Setting

Message

Protagonist

Name

Driving Goal

Obstacle or Conflict

Get writing!

_____
_____
_____
_____
_____
_____
_____
_____
_____
_____
_____
_____
_____
_____

Word Count _____

Title

Themes

Prompt

Setting

Message

Protagonist

Name

Driving Goal

Obstacle or Conflict

Get writing!

Word Count _____

Title

Themes

Prompt

Setting

Message

Protagonist

Name

Driving Goal

Obstacle or Conflict

Get writing!

Word Count

Title

Themes

Prompt

Setting

Message

Protagonist

Name

Driving Goal

Obstacle or Conflict

Get writing!

Word Count _____

Title

Themes

Prompt

Setting

Message

Protagonist

Name

Driving Goal

Obstacle or Conflict

Get writing!

Word Count _____

Title

Themes

Prompt

Setting

Message

Protagonist

Name

Driving Goal

Obstacle or Conflict

Get writing!

Word Count _____

Title

Themes

Prompt

Setting

Message

Protagonist

Name

Driving Goal

Obstacle or Conflict

Get writing!

Word Count

Title

Themes

Prompt

Setting

Message

Protagonist

Name

Driving Goal

Obstacle or Conflict

Get writing!

Word Count _____

Title

Themes

Prompt

Setting

Message

Protagonist

Name

Driving Goal

Obstacle or Conflict

Get writing!

Word Count _____

Title

Themes

Prompt

Setting

Message

Protagonist

Name

Driving Goal

Obstacle or Conflict

Get writing!

Word Count _____

Title

Themes

Prompt

Setting

Message

Protagonist

Name

Driving Goal

Obstacle or Conflict

Get writing!

Word Count _____

Title

Themes

Prompt

Setting

Message

Protagonist

Name

Driving Goal

Obstacle or Conflict

Get writing!

Word Count _____

Title

Themes

Prompt

Setting

Message

Protagonist

Name

Driving Goal

Obstacle or Conflict

Get writing!

Word Count _____

Title

Themes

Prompt

Setting

Message

Protagonist

Name

Driving Goal

Obstacle or Conflict

Get writing!

Word Count

Title

Themes

Prompt

Setting

Message

Protagonist

Name

Driving Goal

Obstacle or Conflict

Get writing!

Word Count _____

Title

Themes

Prompt

Setting

Message

Protagonist

Name

Driving Goal

Obstacle or Conflict

Get writing!

Word Count _____

Title

Themes

Prompt

Setting

Message

Protagonist

Name

Driving Goal

Obstacle or Conflict

Get writing!

Word Count _____

Title

Themes

Prompt

Setting

Message

Protagonist

Name

Driving Goal

Obstacle or Conflict

Get writing!

Word Count _____

Title

Themes

Prompt

Setting

Message

Protagonist

Name

Driving Goal

Obstacle or Conflict

Get writing!

Word Count _____

Title

Themes

Prompt

Setting

Message

Protagonist

Name

Driving Goal

Obstacle or Conflict

Get writing!

Word Count _____

Title

Themes

Prompt

Setting

Message

Protagonist

Name

Driving Goal

Obstacle or Conflict

Get writing!

Word Count _____

Title

Themes

Prompt

Setting

Message

Protagonist

Name

Driving Goal

Obstacle or Conflict

Get writing!

Word Count _____

Title

Themes

Prompt

Setting

Message

Protagonist

Name

Driving Goal

Obstacle or Conflict

Get writing!

Word Count _____

Title

Themes

Prompt

Setting

Message

Protagonist

Name

Driving Goal

Obstacle or Conflict

Get writing!

Word Count _____

Title

Themes

Prompt

Setting

Message

Protagonist

Name

Driving Goal

Obstacle or Conflict

Get writing!

Word Count _____

Title

Themes

Prompt

Setting

Message

Protagonist

Name

Driving Goal

Obstacle or Conflict

Get writing!

Word Count

Title

Themes

Prompt

Setting

Message

Protagonist

Name

Driving Goal

Obstacle or Conflict

Get writing!

Word Count _____

Title

Themes

Prompt

Setting

Message

Protagonist

Name

Driving Goal

Obstacle or Conflict

Get writing!

Word Count _____

Title

Themes

Prompt

Setting

Message

Protagonist

Name

Driving Goal

Obstacle or Conflict

Get writing!

Word Count _____

Title

Themes

Prompt

Setting

Message

Protagonist

Name

Driving Goal

Obstacle or Conflict

Get writing!

Word Count _____

Title

Themes

Prompt

Setting

Message

Protagonist

Name

Driving Goal

Obstacle or Conflict

Get writing!

Word Count _____

Title

Themes

Prompt

Setting

Message

Protagonist

Name

Driving Goal

Obstacle or Conflict

Get writing!

Word Count

Title

Themes

Prompt

Setting

Message

Protagonist

Name

Driving Goal

Obstacle or Conflict

Get writing!

Word Count _____

Title

Themes

Prompt

Setting

Message

Protagonist

Name

Driving Goal

Obstacle or Conflict

Get writing!

Word Count _____

Title

Themes

Prompt

Setting

Message

Protagonist

Name

Driving Goal

Obstacle or Conflict

Get writing!

Word Count _____

Title

Themes

Prompt

Setting

Message

Protagonist

Name

Driving Goal

Obstacle or Conflict

Get writing!

Word Count _____

Title

Themes

Prompt

Setting

Message

Protagonist

Name

Driving Goal

Obstacle or Conflict

Get writing!

_____
_____
_____
_____
_____
_____
_____
_____
_____
_____
_____
_____
_____

Word Count _____

Title

Themes

Prompt

Setting

Message

Protagonist

Name

Driving Goal

Obstacle or Conflict

Get writing!

Word Count _____

Title

Themes

Prompt

Setting

Message

Protagonist

Name

Driving Goal

Obstacle or Conflict

Get writing!

Word Count _____

Title

Themes

Prompt

Setting

Message

Protagonist

Name

Driving Goal

Obstacle or Conflict

Get writing!

Word Count

Title

Themes

Prompt

Setting

Message

Protagonist

Name

Driving Goal

Obstacle or Conflict

Get writing!

Word Count _____

Title

Themes

Prompt

Setting

Message

Protagonist

Name

Driving Goal

Obstacle or Conflict

Get writing!

Word Count _____

Title

Themes

Prompt

Setting

Message

Protagonist

Name

Driving Goal

Obstacle or Conflict

Get writing!

Word Count _____

Title

Themes

Prompt

Setting

Message

Protagonist

Name

Driving Goal

Obstacle or Conflict

Get writing!

Word Count _____

Title

Themes

Prompt

Setting

Message

Protagonist

Name

Driving Goal

Obstacle or Conflict

Get writing!

Word Count _____

Title

Themes

Prompt

Setting

Message

Protagonist

Name

Driving Goal

Obstacle or Conflict

Get writing!

Word Count _____

Title

Themes

Prompt

Setting

Message

Protagonist

Name

Driving Goal

Obstacle or Conflict

Get writing!

Word Count _____

Title

Themes

Prompt

Setting

Message

Protagonist

Name

Driving Goal

Obstacle or Conflict

Get writing!

Word Count _____

Title

Themes

Prompt

Setting

Message

Protagonist

Name

Driving Goal

Obstacle or Conflict

Get writing!

Word Count _____

Title

Themes

Prompt

Setting

Message

Protagonist

Name

Driving Goal

Obstacle or Conflict

Get writing!

Word Count _____

Title

Themes

Prompt

Setting

Message

Protagonist

Name

Driving Goal

Obstacle or Conflict

Get writing!

Word Count _____

Title

Themes

Prompt

Setting

Message

Protagonist

Name

Driving Goal

Obstacle or Conflict

Get writing!

Word Count

Title

Themes

Prompt

Setting

Message

Protagonist

Name

Driving Goal

Obstacle or Conflict

Get writing!

Word Count _____

Title

Themes

Prompt

Setting

Message

Protagonist

Name

Driving Goal

Obstacle or Conflict

Get writing!

Word Count _____

Title

Themes

Prompt

Setting

Message

Protagonist

Name

Driving Goal

Obstacle or Conflict

Get writing!

Word Count _____

Title

Themes

Prompt

Setting

Message

Protagonist

Name

Driving Goal

Obstacle or Conflict

Get writing!

Word Count _____

Title

Themes

Prompt

Setting

Message

Protagonist

Name

Driving Goal

Obstacle or Conflict

Get writing!

Word Count _____

Title

Themes

Prompt

Setting

Message

Protagonist

Name

Driving Goal

Obstacle or Conflict

Get writing!

Word Count _____

Title

Themes

Prompt

Setting

Message

Protagonist

Name

Driving Goal

Obstacle or Conflict

Get writing!

Word Count _____

Title

Themes

Prompt

Setting

Message

Protagonist

Name

Driving Goal

Obstacle or Conflict

Get writing!

Word Count _____

Title

Themes

Prompt

Setting

Message

Protagonist

Name

Driving Goal

Obstacle or Conflict

Get writing!

Word Count _____

Title

Themes

Prompt

Setting

Message

Protagonist

Name

Driving Goal

Obstacle or Conflict

Get writing!

Word Count

Title

Themes

Prompt

Setting

Message

Protagonist

Name

Driving Goal

Obstacle or Conflict

Get writing!

Word Count _____

Title

Themes

Prompt

Setting

Message

Protagonist

Name

Driving Goal

Obstacle or Conflict

Get writing!

Word Count _____

Title

Themes

Prompt

Setting

Message

Protagonist

Name

Driving Goal

Obstacle or Conflict

Get writing!

_____
_____
_____
_____
_____
_____
_____
_____
_____
_____
_____
_____

Word Count _____

Title

Themes

Prompt

Setting

Message

Protagonist

Name

Driving Goal

Obstacle or Conflict

Get writing!

Word Count _____

Title

Themes

Prompt

Setting

Message

Protagonist

Name

Driving Goal

Obstacle or Conflict

Get writing!

Word Count _____

Title

Themes

Prompt

Setting

Message

Protagonist

Name

Driving Goal

Obstacle or Conflict

Get writing!

Word Count _____

Title

Themes

Prompt

Setting

Message

Protagonist

Name

Driving Goal

Obstacle or Conflict

Get writing!

_____
_____
_____
_____
_____
_____
_____
_____
_____
_____
_____
_____
_____

Word Count _____

Title

Themes

Prompt

Setting

Message

Protagonist

Name

Driving Goal

Obstacle or Conflict

Get writing!

Word Count _____

Title

Themes

Prompt

Setting

Message

Protagonist

Name

Driving Goal

Obstacle or Conflict

Get writing!

Word Count _____

Title

Themes

Prompt

Setting

Message

Protagonist

Name

Driving Goal

Obstacle or Conflict

Get writing!

Word Count _____

Title

Themes

Prompt

Setting

Message

Protagonist

Name

Driving Goal

Obstacle or Conflict

Get writing!

Word Count _____

Title

Themes

Prompt

Setting

Message

Protagonist

Name

Driving Goal

Obstacle or Conflict

Get writing!

Word Count _____

Title

Themes

Prompt

Setting

Message

Protagonist

Name

Driving Goal

Obstacle or Conflict

Get writing!

_____
_____
_____
_____
_____
_____
_____
_____
_____
_____
_____
_____
_____
_____
_____
_____

Word Count _____

Title

Themes

Prompt

Setting

Message

Protagonist

Name

Driving Goal

Obstacle or Conflict

Get writing!

Word Count

Title

Themes

Prompt

Setting

Message

Protagonist

Name

Driving Goal

Obstacle or Conflict

Get writing!

Word Count _____

Title

Themes

Prompt

Setting

Message

Protagonist

Name

Driving Goal

Obstacle or Conflict

Get writing!

Word Count

Title

Themes

Prompt

Setting

Message

Protagonist

Name

Driving Goal

Obstacle or Conflict

Get writing!

Word Count _____

Title

Themes

Prompt

Setting

Message

Protagonist

Name

Driving Goal

Obstacle or Conflict

Get writing!

Word Count _____

Title

Themes

Prompt

Setting

Message

Protagonist

Name

Driving Goal

Obstacle or Conflict

Get writing!

Word Count _____

www.ingramcontent.com/pod-product-compliance
Lightning Source LLC
LaVergne TN
LVHW012116070526
838202LV00056B/5750